W9-ANM-991

Sammy Seal OF THE CIRCUS

BY CATHRINE BARR

NEW YORK OXFORD UNIVERSITY PRESS 1955

Library of Congress Catalog Card Number 55-10427

SECOND PRINTING 1956

PRINTED IN THE UNITED STATES OF AMERICA

Sammy Seal
of the Circus was afraid to go into the center ring. He could not do tricks like the other seals. He watched sadly from the wing with Joey.

Joey, the gay clown, didn't like to have Sammy so sad. He reached for Sammy and began to keep time to the band music.

Soon they were dancing to the merry rhythm. Boom went the drums! Joey kicked high, and a bell came off his shoe. Away it went!

Sammy danced after it and bounced it up on his nose.

Back and forth he danced, bouncing the bell.
What fun! He missed, and the bell rolled away.

But Sammy Seal soon had it bouncing again.

Sammy danced and bounced the bell. Way to the side he stretched . .

. . . . .far back. . . . . .

. . . .way forward !

Sammy stood on just one flipper. But
he never missed the bell.

Suddenly Joey tossed in an orange. Sammy leaned out and bounced the orange too, then the bell, then the orange.

Ooops! He missed! But he started right in again, for now he knew what fun it was to bounce the bell and orange together.

One afternoon as
Sammy danced with the
bell and orange, he began to
spin. Just then Joey threw him a coconut.

Sammy caught that too! Away he twirled as he bounced the bell, the orange, and the coconut. Over and over, faster and faster. Joey watched and gaily beat time.

Then one day the toys were lost!
Sammy searched everywhere.

At last he saw the bell in the sawdust and hurried to get it.

As he bounced it from his nose he
saw the orange ahead.

The coconut wasn't far off, and soon Sammy was bouncing all three.

He was so glad he had found his toys.
He bounced them higher and faster than ever.

He did not look to either side until he
came to Joey, who was beating time.

Suddenly a big spotlight shone on them.

There was a loud cheer.

Sammy Seal had danced right into the center ring. The circus crowd was all around.

But what fun he was having! He danced on, spinning fast and bouncing the bell and the orange and the coconut. The crowd cheered.

. . . . and cheered.

Joey beamed and beat time.

Sammy was happy. His eyes sparkled and twinkled.

After that was Sammy Seal sad and afraid?
Never again!